W9-BXC-105

Young Justice™

5

STONE ARCH BOOKS
a capstone imprint

STONE ARCH BOOKS™

ublished in 2013
 Capstone Imprint
710 Roe Crest Drive
orth Mankato, MN 56003
ww.capstonepub.com

riginally published by DC Comics in the U.S. in single
magazine form as Young Justice #5.

C Comics
700 Broadway, New York, NY 10019
 Warner Bros. Entertainment Company

rinted in China by Nordica.
413/CA21300442
32013 007226NORDF13

ataloging-in-Publication Data is available at the
ibrary of Congress website:
SBN: 978-1-4342-6037-6 (library binding)

ummary: Aqualad, Robin, Kid Flash, Superboy
and Miss Martian are ready for their first
mission as a team. To get to know each other
etter, they decide to trade stories around the
ampfire, revealing how they all started as
rimefighters. Will this bring them together or
nderscore their differences?

TONE ARCH BOOKS

shley C. Andersen Zantop *Publisher*
Michael Dahl *Editorial Director*
onald Lemke & Sean Tulien *Editors*
eather Kindseth *Creative Director*
rann Garvey & Alison Thiele *Designers*
athy McColley *Production Specialist*

C COMICS

cott Peterson & Jim Chadwick *Original U.S. Editors*
Michael McCalister *U.S. Assistant Editor*
Mike Norton *Cover Artist*

YOUNG JUSTICE
CAMPFIRE SECRETS
Art Baltazar .... writer
Franco .... writer
Christopher Jones .... artist
Zac Atkinson ....colorist
Carlos M. Mangual .... letterer

YOUNG JUSTICE™

AQUALAD

AGE: 16 SECRET IDENTITY: Kaldur' Ahm

BIO: Aquaman's apprentice; a cool, calm warrior and leader; totally amphibious with the ability to bend and shape water.

SUPERBOY

AGE: 16 SECRET IDENTITY: Conner Kent

BIO: Cloned from Superman; a shy and uncertain teenager; gifted with super-strength, infrared vision, and leaping abilities.

ARTEMIS

AGE: 15 SECRET IDENTITY: Classified

BIO: Green Arrow's niece; a dedicated and tough fighter; extremely talented in both archery and martial arts.

KID FLASH

AGE: 15 SECRET IDENTITY: Wally West

BIO: Partner of the Flash; a competitive team member, often lacking self-control; gifted with super-speed.

ROBIN

AGE: 13 SECRET IDENTITY: Dick Grayson

BIO: Partner of Batman; the youngest member of the team; talented acrobat, martial artist, and hacker.

MISS MARTIAN

AGE: 16 SECRET IDENTITY: M'gann M'orzz

BIO: Martian Manhunter's niece; polite and sweet; ability to shape-shift, read minds, transform, and fly.

THE STORY SO FAR...

Kid Flash tries to get Miss Martian alone for a campfire retreat, but the other Young Justice members decide to tag along...

MOUNT JUSTICE.
JULY 20, 21:32 EDT

CH 099

SEEN IT. SEEN IT. SEEN IT. SEEN IT. DON'T WANT TO SEE IT.

BORING. DON'T OWN ANY STOCKS. ALREADY GOT A *SLAP CHOP*. SEEN IT. SEEN IT. SEEN IT.

I CAN'T BELIEVE WE GET *SIX HUNDRED* CHANNELS ON THIS THING AND THERE'S *NOTHING* ON.

!

HEY THERE.

OH. HELLO, WALLY.

HEY! ARE YOU BUSY?... UHHH... I MEAN...
WHAT'S GOING ON?
NOT MUCH. I WAS JUST GOING TO MAKE A SANDWICH. WOULD YOU LIKE ONE?

OH. NO, THANKS.
BESIDES, I PRETTY MUCH CLEANED OUT EVERYTHING THAT WAS IN HERE ANYWAY.

WHICH REMINDS ME, SOMEONE *NEEDS* TO GO SHOPPING. YOU GOT ANYTHING PLANNED FOR TONIGHT?
NO. I WAS JUST PLANNING ON HANGING AROUND THE CAVE TONIGHT.

OH, REALLY? THAT'S COOL! HEY... UHM... HERE'S AN IDEA, DO YOU, LIKE, WANT TO GO TO THE MOVIES?
SURE I WOULD LOVE TO!
BUT... I DON'T HAVE ANY MONEY.

OH.
ME NEITHER.

HOW ABOUT *SURFING*? DO YOU WANT TO GO SURFING? YOU AND I CAN HIT THE WAVES, I COULD TEACH YOU HOW TO SURF *KID FLASH* STYLE!
WOULDN'T IT BE BETTER IN THE *DAYTIME*?
OH... I GUESS YOU'RE RIGHT, PROBABLY TOO DARK OUT.

THERE'S A FULL MOON OUT TONIGHT. WANT TO SIT OUTSIDE AND LOOK AT THE STARS?
OH. *THAT* SOUNDS NICE.
GREAT! WE CAN BUILD A *FIRE* AND EVERYTHING.
OH! *A FIRE?*

YEAH, YOU KNOW, A NICE *ROARING* CAMPFIRE... OH, WAIT, SORRY, I FORGOT.
NO. IT'S OKAY. AS LONG AS I DON'T HAVE TO SIT TOO CLOSE...
GREAT! TONIGHT WOULD BE *PERFECT!* WE CAN ROAST MARSHMALLOWS AND EVERYTHING!
MARSHMALLOWS? I'VE *NEVER* HAD A MARSHMALLOW BEFORE!

WE CAN MAKE S'MORES. YOU KNOW, WITH GRAHAM CRACKERS, CHOCOLATE AND STUFF.
I'VE *HEARD* OF THEM BUT NEVER HAD ONE. CAN WE MAKE *THOSE?*

WHAT DO *YOU* THINK?
YES!

GREAT!
OH! THIS IS GOING TO BE VERY EXCITING!
GIVE ME A FEW MINUTES AND I'LL GRAB SOME THINGS AND WE CAN GO.
A FEW MINUTES LATER.
...GATHERED A COUPLE OF CHAIRS, SOME FIREWOOD, SCROUNGED THE PANTRY FOR GRAHAM CRACKERS, CHOCOLATE AND MARSHMALLOWS AND NOW WE'LL COZY UP TOGETHER OUTSIDE--
--JUST THE TWO OF US?
WE'RE GOING TO NEED A LOT MORE STUFF THAN THAT IF WE'RE GONNA GO CAMPING!
I HOPE YOU DON'T MIND, I INVITED ALL THE OTHERS TO JOIN IN THE FUN WITH THE S'MORES!

THIS WAS A GREAT IDEA, DON'T YOU THINK WALLY? CAMPING IN THE GREAT OUTDOORS!
I DON'T REMEMBER INVITING YOU. BESIDES, I DIDN'T SAY ANYTHING ABOUT CAMPING. I SAID A CAMP FIRE. BIG DIFFERENCE BETWEEN JUST A CAMPFIRE AND THE WHOLE CAMPING THING. I DON'T LIKE CAMPING... OUTSIDE...
UNLESS OF COURSE I'M CAMPING WITH THAT SPECIAL SOMEONE.
DUDE, KINDA BORDERING ON CREEPY.
WELL, I THINK ALL OF US CAMPING IS A WONDERFUL IDEA!
SHE DOESN'T SEEM TO THINK SO.
SHE'S PROBABLY ON A SUGAR OVERLOAD.
THANKS TO WALLY, I GET TO TRY S'MORES FOR THE FIRST TIME!
WHAT CAN I SAY? I'M A SWEETIE! HA! GET IT? CAUSE S'MORES ARE SWEET?

SO, THIS IS WHAT YOU DO WHEN YOU GO CAMPING?
SLEEP IN THESE FLIMSY THINGS CALLED "TENTS" AND SIT AROUND THE FIRE?
YEAH, THAT'S PRETTY MUCH ABOUT IT SO IF YOU FEEL LIKE HEADING HOME I CAN SIT OUT HERE WITH MS. M... ALONE.
YOU'RE ABOUT AS SUBTLE AS A TRAIN WRECK, YOU KNOW THAT?
YOU'RE NOT GOING TO CATCH ANY FISH UNLESS YOU GO FISHING DUDE.
SORRY. NO OFFENSE.
NO, USUALLY YOU SIT AROUND THE CAMPFIRE AND TELL STORIES.
OH!
I WOULD LOVE TO HEAR YOUR STORY, KALDUR. COULD YOU TELL US HOW YOU BECAME AQUALAD?
I WAS THINKING MORE OF A GHOST STORY TYPE OF THING BUT I GUESS... WHATEVER.

OH. I SUPPOSE I COULD DO THAT IF YOU DO NOT THINK IT WILL BE TOO BORING.
NOT AT ALL! I WOULD LOVE TO HEAR IT!
WELL, I GREW UP IN THE CITY OF SHAYERIS, WHICH IS A CITY IN ATLANTIS. SURFACE DWELLERS THINK ALL ATLANTEANS ARE THE SAME, BUT OUR KINGDOM HAS MANY CITIES, MANY PEOPLE, MANY CULTURES.
WHEN I WAS TWELVE, I COMPLETED MY EDUCATION AND BEGAN MY MANDATORY SERVICE IN THE ATLANTEAN MILITARY, WHICH IS STANDARD FOR ALL AT THAT AGE. AFTER A WHILE I WAS TRANSFERRED TO THE PRESTIGIOUS CONSERVATORY OF SORCERY IN THE ATLANTEAN CAPITAL OF POSEIDONIS.
"QUEEN MERA IS THE HEAD MISTRESS OF THE CONSERVATORY AND WIFE OF KING ORIN, AQUAMAN."
"IT WAS A VERY DIFFERENT TIME FOR ME.
"IT WAS DIFFICULT, AS IT WOULD BE FOR ANYONE AT AGE FOURTEEN I SUPPOSE, BUT ALSO A TIME IN MY LIFE WHERE I MET FRIENDS THAT I KNOW WILL BE WITH ME FOR A LIFETIME.
"THEN CAME A DAY... A HORRIBLE DAY WHEN POSEIDONIS WAS ATTACKED BY THE OCEAN MASTER. I CAN REMEMBER IT VIVIDLY, AS IF IT HAPPENED ONLY YESTERDAY.
"IT WAS THE DAY AQUAMAN NEARLY MET HIS END.
"AQUAMAN AND OCEAN MASTER FOUGHT FOR WHAT SEEMED LIKE HOURS.
"WHEN AQUAMAN AND OCEAN MASTER CLASHED, IT SEEMED TO SHAKE THE VERY FOUNDATIONS OF THE CITY."

"OCEAN MASTER HAD GAINED THE UPPER HAND AND NEARLY DEFEATED AQUAMAN.
"CORRECTION.
"AQUAMAN *WAS* DEFEATED.
"GARTH, A FELLOW STUDENT, AND I INTERVENED ON THE KING'S BEHALF.
"IT WAS THE ONLY THING WE COULD THINK OF DOING. THE DANGER DID NOT OCCUR TO US, THE ONLY THING THAT MATTERED TO US AT THE TIME WAS THAT OUR KING WAS IN TROUBLE.
"IT MAY HAVE BEEN ONE OF THE MOST FOOLISH THINGS GARTH AND I HAD EVER DONE, AS WE NEARLY MET OUR OWN END.
"WE HAD NO HOPE OF DEFEATING HIM WHATSOEVER, BUT THE TIME WE SPENT ENGAGED IN BATTLE AGAINST THE OCEAN MASTER WAS TIME ENOUGH FOR OUR KING TO RECOVER.
"THAT WAS ALL HE NEEDED AS AQUAMAN FINALLY *TRIUMPHED* OVER OCEAN MASTER!
"HE WAS ABLE TO DRIVE HIM AWAY FROM THE CITY AND SAVE US ALL!"

"AQUAMAN IS A BEING OF TWO WORLDS. ON THE SURFACE WORLD HE FIGHTS FOR JUSTICE FOR ALL BEINGS. UNDER THE SEA HE IS A LEADER TO MANY. BOTH CARRY THE WEIGHT OF RESPONSIBILITIES. OVERWHELMING RESPONSIBILITIES ONLY EVEN THE BEST OF MEN CAN CARRY FOR SO LONG.
"EVEN AQUAMAN CANNOT DO BOTH FOREVER.

"REALIZING THAT ON THE SURFACE BOTH BATMAN AND GREEN ARROW HAD TAKEN ON *APPRENTICES* THAT COULD ONE DAY TAKE OVER THEIR RESPECTIVE MANTELS, KING ORIN HAD BEEN CONTEMPLATING THE SAME IDEA.

"WITH THIS IN MIND, HE APPROACHED BOTH GARTH AND MYSELF WITH THE POSSIBILITY OF BECOMING HIS PROTÉGÉS.
"I MUST ADMIT THE POSSIBILITY INTRIGUED ME IMMEDIATELY.

"I HAD NEVER BEEN TO THE SURFACE WORLD. AND I AM THE FIRST TO ADMIT THAT I AM A BIT OF AN ADVENTURER. MANY IS THE DAY IN CLASS THAT I WOULD DREAM OF VISITING DISTANT OCEANS AND POSSIBLY ONE DAY EVEN THE SURFACE WORLD.
"BOTH GARTH AND I *SERIOUSLY* CONSIDERED THE KING'S OFFER.

"GARTH ULTIMATELY CHOSE TO CONTINUE HIS STUDIES WITH QUEEN MERA AT THE CONSERVATORY OF SORCERY.
"FOR ME, HOWEVER, THE CHANCE TO VISIT THE SURFACE WORLD WAS A DREAM COME TRUE."

"SO AT THE AGE OF FOURTEEN, I BECAME AQUALAD.
"I MISS MY FRIENDS. GARTH. TULA...
"BUT THE CHANCE TO WORK WITH MY MENTOR AND KING WAS AN OPPORTUNITY I COULD NOT PASS UP. I LIKE TO THINK THE WORK I AM DOING MAKES A DIFFERENCE."
THE REST OF THE STORY YOU KNOW. AQUAMAN BROUGHT AQUALAD TO THE SURFACE WORLD... AND NOW I AM HERE WITH YOU.
WOW, SO YOU *WANTED* TO BE AQUALAD?
YES. THE OPPORTUNITY AROSE. I COULD THINK OF NO OTHER PATH.
YEAH? IF YOU THINK *HE* WANTED TO BE AQUALAD SO BAD? LET ME TELL YOU ABOUT HOW *I* GOT STARTED.
"IT LITERALLY GOES BACK A COUPLE OF GENERATIONS...
"EACH GENERATION OF *FLASH* STARTED WITH A *BANG*! LITERALLY!
"JAY GARRICK WAS IN A FREAK LAB ACCIDENT.
"BOOM! THERE IT IS!"
LAMPCRT

"DURING THE 40'S AND THE 50'S HE WAS EVERYWHERE!
"THE FASTEST MAN ALIVE!
"JAY GARRICK WAS THE WORLD'S FIRST *FLASH*!
"THEN ONE DAY THIS GUY COMES ALONG, A HUGE FAN OF THE FLASH, WANTING TO KNOW ALL ABOUT THIS JAY GARRICK, BACK IN THOSE DAYS JAY DIDN'T REALLY HIDE HIS IDENTITY.
"HE CONTACTS JAY AND THE TWO SPEND HOURS AND HOURS TALKING ABOUT HIS ADVENTURES AND ABOUT THE ACCIDENT THAT TURNED HIM INTO THE FLASH.
"THIS GUY EVEN GOES SO FAR AS TO *RE-CREATE* THE ACCIDENT THAT CREATED THE ORIGINAL.
BUT WHERE JAY GARRICK'S ACCIDENT WAS A TOTAL FREAK THING, THIS GUY RECREATED THE ACCIDENT UNDER LABORATORY CONDITIONS. HE SET THE WHOLE THING UP IN A LAB AND *TRIED* TO MAKE IT HAPPEN!
"RESULT? STILL A BIG EXPLOSION! BUT, LO AND BEHOLD HE BECOMES SPEEDY MCSPEED-SPEED HIMSELF!
"NOW HE'S THE *FLASH*! WELL, NOT THE ORIGINAL FLASH BUT THE NEW FLASH... THE FLASH WE ALL KNOW!
"I MEAN, THERE'S THE JAY GARRICK FLASH AND NOW THERE'S THE NEW FLASH. YOU KNOW, IT JUST OCCURRED TO ME THAT THEY COULD PROBABLY USE DIFFERENT NAMES. ANYWAY...
"...THIS TIME HE'S EVEN FASTER THAN FLASH, WELL, THE OLD FLASH... IT GAVE HIM EVEN *MORE* SPEED!"

OKAY, SO CHECK THIS! THE SECOND FLASH IS A FAN OF THE FIRST FLASH--JAY GARRICK. IT TURNS OUT GREAT MINDS THINK ALIKE, CAUSE I WAS A FAN OF THE FLASH--THE SECOND ONE, NOT THE FIRST ONE.
WELL, I WAS A FAN OF JAY GARRICK, THE FIRST ONE AFTER I GOT TO KNOW HIM. HE WAS A LITTLE BEFORE MY TIME.
"LONG STORY SHORT, ONE DAY I WAS IN MY UNCLE'S HOUSE, STUMBLED ACROSS HIS NOTEBOOKS AND GOT THE SHOCK OF A LIFE-TIME!
"THAT WAS THE DAY I FOUND OUT MY UNCLE WAS *THE FLASH!*
"ONCE THE SHOCK PASSED A BIT, I KEPT READING. HE WAS KEEPING A JOURNAL OF ALL HIS EXPERIENCES AND EXPERIMENTS! ESPECIALLY THE ONE THAT MADE HIM THE FLASH, THE SECOND ONE, NOT THE FIRST--"
"WE GET IT ALREADY!"
"WHEN I FOUND *THAT* OUT, I WOULD KIND OF KEEP HINTING TO MY UNCLE THAT THE FLASH COULD MAYBE USE A PARTNER.
NO!
WHAT? WHY?
"I TRIED TO CONVINCE HIM THAT FLASH COULD *USE* AND PROBABLY *NEEDED* A PARTNER.
"I MEAN COME ON, BY THIS TIME BATS ALREADY HAD ROBBIE OVER HERE AND GREEN ARROW HAD SPEEDY! THIS WAS A NO-BRAINER!
"I'VE GOT TO ADMIT, FLASH WAS A BIT RESISTANT AT FIRST.
NO! NO PARTNERS!
I DON'T WANT THE RESPONSIBILITY.
DOES THIS SOUND CONFUSING TO ANYONE ELSE?

JUST LET ME FINISH AND YOU WILL BE CONFUSED NO MORE, SUPEY.
SO, HAVING SEEN HIS JOURNAL JUST LIKE HE SAW THE PREVIOUS FLASH'S, I TRY TO RE-CREATE THE EXPERIMENT WITH MY *OWN* CHEMISTRY SET.
"AND WHAT DO YOU KNOW? I WAS ABLE TO DO IT!"
BOOM
WEST
THE EXPERIMENT ACTUALLY WORKED?
WELL...

HOSPITAL
"NOT AT FIRST, ACTUALLY.
THIS IS NOT YOUR FAULT.
THEY WERE MY NOTES, IRIS. OF COURSE THIS IS MY FAULT.
"IT DIDN'T HAPPEN AT FIRST, BUT A COUPLE OF WEEKS LATER... I WAS OFF AND RUNNING.
"I COULDN'T WAIT TO SHOW FLASH!
"WHEN HE SAW THAT I HAD POWERS, HOW COULD HE NOT WANT ME AS A PARTNER?
"YOU GUYS SHOULD'VE SEEN HIS FACE WHEN I SHOWED HIM!"
I CAN BE YOUR PARTNER! WE WOULD MAKE A GREAT TEAM!
I COULD BE...KID FLASH!

"THIS TIME HE JUMPED AT THE CHANCE TO HAVE A PARTNER!
"FLASH COULDN'T WAIT TO SHOW THE WORLD!
OKAY.... YOU CAN BE KID FLASH. BUT YOU DO EXACTLY AS I SAY, WHEN I SAY IT.
"THE FLASH WAS BEYOND ECSTATIC! HE COULDN'T CONTAIN HIS EXCITEMENT! IT WAS THE GREATEST DAY IN THE HISTORY OF THE WORLD!
"WHY, YOU ASK?
JUST FOR THE RECORD, WE DIDN'T.
"THAT'S THE DAY THE WORLD GOT KID FLASH!"
YOU.
ARE.
WELCOME.

YEAH. WE'RE ALL THRILLED YOU'RE SO SPEED-CAPABLE.
WHAT'S THE MATTER? *JEALOUS?*
SHEEYEAH, *RIGHT!* JEALOUS OF *YOU?*
CAN YOU TELL US ABOUT HOW YOU GOT STARTED, ROBIN?
HAHA! *SNORT*
ARE YOU *KIDDING* ME? *BATS* WON'T EVEN LET HIM TELL YOU HIS REAL NAME!

HAHAHAHA!
I MEAN...
YOU'LL PROBABLY GET A BETTER ORIGIN STORY OUT OF SUPEY OVER HERE.
BUT YOU ALREADY TOLD ME HIS STORY. DIDN'T YOU? YOU SAID THAT THE THREE OF YOU RESCUED HIM FROM CADMUS.
YEAH, WE DID.
YES. CHRONOLOGICALLY, SUPERBOY IS ONLY 16 WEEKS OLD.
...AND YOU HAVE NO MEMORY OF THINGS BEFORE BEING RESCUED?

I HAVE SOME MEMORIES...FROM THE G-GNOME.
IT WOULD TEACH ME ABOUT THE WORLD OUTSIDE WHILE I WAS IN THE CONTAINMENT POD.
SO YOU CAN REMEMBER THINGS? WHEN YOU WERE IN THE CONTAINMENT POD THEY WOULD FEED YOU INFORMATION AND YOU COULD REMEMBER IT, RIGHT?
I GUESS SO.
WELL IF YOU CAN REMEMBER WHAT THEY TAUGHT YOU, YOU MUST'VE BEEN THINKING ABOUT THINGS AS THEY FED YOU INFORMATION. WHAT DID YOU THINK ABOUT?
WHEN I WAS IN THE CONTAINMENT POD, I WAS FED...
...INFORMATION.

I REALLY DIDN'T START THINKING FOR MYSELF UNTIL AFTER I GOT OUT.
WELL, WHAT KIND OF THINGS DO YOU THINK ABOUT NOW?
THE *ONE* THING...
THAT'S *ALWAYS* ON MY MIND...
IS...

DESTROYING SUPERMAN.
WHAT'S THE STORY?
WRITTEN BY ART BALTAZAR AND FRANCO
ART BY CHRISTOPHER JONES
COLORED BY ZAC ATKINSON
LETTERED BY CARLOS M. MANGUAL
COVER BY MIKE NORTON AND ALEX SINCLAIR
ASSISTANT EDITING BY MICHAEL MCCALISTER
EDITED BY JIM CHADWICK
TO BE CONTINUED...

CAN YOUNG JUSTICE TURN THINGS AROUND...?

Read the next action-packed adventure to find out!

CREATORS

ART BALTAZAR WRITER

Art Baltazar is a cartoonist machine from the heart of Chicago! He defines cartoons and comics not only as an art style, but as a way of life. Currently, Art is the creative force behind *The New York Times* best-selling, Eisner Award-winning, DC Comics series Tiny Titans, and the co-writer for Billy Batson and the Magic of SHAZAM! and co-creator of Superman Family Adventures. Art is living the dream! He draws comics and never has to leave the house. He lives with his lovely wife, Rose, big boy Sonny, little boy Gordon, and little girl Audrey. Right on!

FRANCO AURELIANI WRITER

Bronx, New York born writer and artist Franco Aureliani has been drawing comics since he could hold a crayon. Currently residing in upstate New York with his wife, Ivette, and son, Nicolas, Franco spends most of his days in a Batcave-like studio where he produces DC's Tiny Titans comics. In 1995, Franco founded Blindwolf Studios, an independent art studio where he and fellow creators can create children's comics. Franco is the creator, artist, and writer of Weirdsville, L'il Creeps, and Eagle All Star, as well as the co-creator and writer of Patrick the Wolf Boy. When he's not writing and drawing, Franco also teaches high school art.

CHRISTOPHER JONES ARTIST

Christopher Jones is a professional illustrator and comic book artist. He has worked on Young Justice, The Batman Strikes!, and many other book series for DC Comics.

GLOSSARY

chronologically (kron-uh-LOJ-uh-kuhl-ee)--arranged in the order of time

containment (kuhn-TAYN-muhnt)--a surrounding enclosure

flimsy (FLIM-zee)--thin or weak

mandatory (MAN-duh-tor-ee)--required by law or custom

overload (oh-vur-LODE)--if you overload something, you give it too much to handle

overwhelming (oh-vur-WELL-ming)--defeating or overcoming completely

prestigious (pre-STEEJ-uhss)--honorable and impressive

sorcery (SORE-suh-ree)--the art or practice of casting spells or using magic

subtle (SUHT-uhl)--faint or delicate, or clever or disguised

triumphed (TRYE-umphd)--earned a great victory or success, or defeated an opponent

ultimately (UHL-ti-mit-lee)--in the end

VISUAL QUESTIONS & PROMPTS

1. In this panel, Robin's head has a red circle around it to separate it from the rest of the panel. Why do you think this was done?

2. Why do you think Kid Flash is disappointed that the others decided to join him and Miss Martian on their trip?

3. These two panels show that Kid Flash isn't entirely trustworthy. In what way does the grown-up Flash's reactions show that Kid Flash is lying a little?

4. Of all the superpowers used in this book, which one would you want for yourself? Why?

"IT DIDN'T HAPPEN AT FIRST, BUT A COUPLE OF WEEKS LATER... I WAS *OFF* AND *RUNNING*.
5

5. Why is the narration box in the panel to the right different colors than the rest? Check the rest of page 18 for clues.

THERE'S A FULL MOON OUT TONIGHT. WANT TO SIT OUTSIDE AND LOOK AT THE STARS?
OH. *THAT* SOUNDS NICE.
GREAT! WE CAN BUILD A *FIRE* AND EVERY-THING.
OH! *A FIRE*?

6. Describe Miss Martian and Kid Flash's emotional states in your own words for each of the four panels to the left.

YEAH, YOU KNOW, A NICE *ROARING* CAMPFIRE... OH, WAIT, SORRY, I FORGOT.
NO. IT'S OKAY. AS LONG AS I DON'T HAVE TO SIT TOO CLOSE...

GREAT! TONIGHT WOULD BE *PERFECT!* WE CAN ROAST MARSHMALLOWS AND EVERYTHING!
MARSHMALLOWS? I'VE *NEVER* HAD A MARSHMALLOW BEFORE!

YOUNG JUSTICE™

READ THEM ALL!

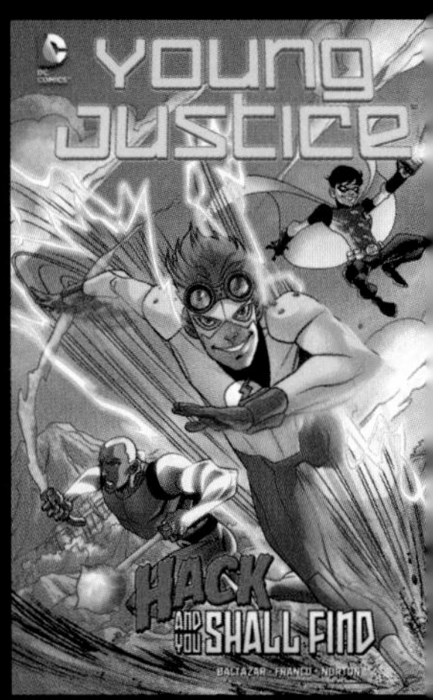

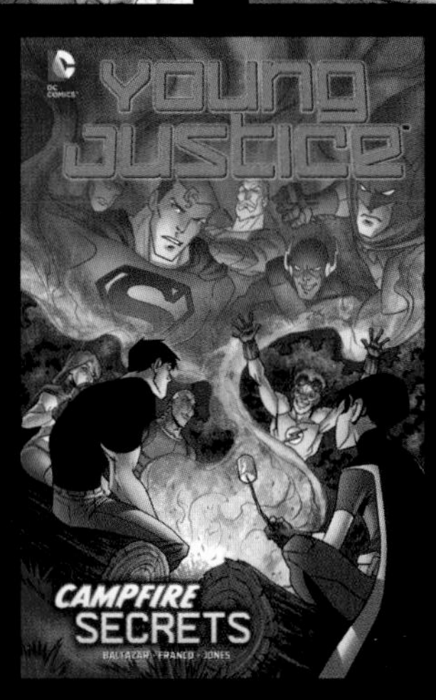

YOUNG JUSTICE™